Harry and Toto

Quiet and Loud

For Calum & Andrew

Adapted by **Jill Findlay**
Created by **Paul Shuttleworth**

Based on the TV series Harry and Toto
and the TV Script "Quiet and Loud", written by Trevor Ricketts
performed by Bob Golding and Sue Devaney
with the music of Liz Kitchen

Original design by
Marcin Wasilewski
Robert Jaszczurowski
Łukasz Kacprowicz

Additional design and book layout by
SunHouse Creative

With special thanks to Loretta
together

There are always lots of different sounds in Opposite Town.

Ding Dong!

TOOT!

"Delivery!"

That's Horace the Horse calling. He has some new books for Lino the Lion who runs the library.

And what's that sound?

"Ice creams, get your ice creams," calls Patrick the Penguin.

Clang! Clang! Clang!

The fire station alarm warns Eric the Elephant of an emergency.

Nee-nar, Nee-nar, Nee-nar!

"I'm on my way," shouts Opposite Town's Firefighter.
The fire engine's siren is very **LOUD!**

Toto the Tortoise doesn't like loud noises.
He's listening to some quiet music on the radio.

"Ah, time for a nap," he thinks.

Toto is just dozing off when....

Bang!
CRASH!
Toot!

Toto gets such a surprise, he spills his milkshake. "Oh what a loud noise," he says, "I really don't like it."

The noise is so loud you can hear it all over Opposite Town. Toto sets off to find out what is spoiling his peace and quiet.

Where do you think the noise is coming from?

Toot! Boom!
CRASH!

The closer Toto gets to his friend Harry's house, the louder the noise becomes.

"Harry the Hare," mutters Toto. "I might have known."

When Harry opens the door,
Toto gets a big surprise.

Harry is playing lots of different instruments all at the same time. "It's my One Hare Band," laughs Harry. "Fabulous, isn't it?"

How many instruments is Harry playing?

Tambourine

Drum

Bells

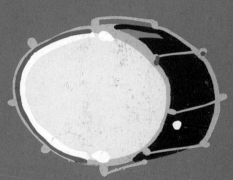

Cymbal

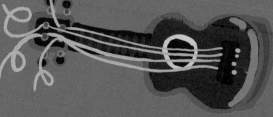

Guitar

Trumpet

He plays all the way to Toto's house, but Toto makes Harry take the instruments off.

"No loud noises in my house," grumbles Toto.

Harry doesn't know what to do without his instruments.

"Just sit quietly and I'll make some milkshakes," says Toto.

But Harry isn't very good at sitting quietly.

He switches the radio on...

...and turns the volume to **LOUD!**

"It's too loud," moans Toto. Harry doesn't agree and swings his friend around to the music.

Toto is annoyed with Harry. He finds some earmuffs to wear so he can't hear the loud music anymore.

"Why can't you do something quiet for a change?" suggests Toto. "Try reading a book."

Now it's your turn to help.

Harry needs to find a book to read.
Who do you think can help?

Is it Patrick the Penguin,
Eric the Elephant
or Lino the Lion?

Who runs the Opposite Town Library?

It's Lino the Lion.

Harry rushes all the way to the library.

"Hello Lino!" he shouts.

"Shh, not so loud Harry," whispers Lino.
"You need to be quiet in the library."

"Why?" asks Harry.

"So that everyone can read their stories in peace," explains Lino.

"Ooh, I love stories," says Harry.

Lino hands Harry a book full
of words and pictures.

Harry tries to read quietly,
but he just can't help being loud.

There are funny bits...
"Ha Ha Ha!"

There are shocking bits...
"Oooh!"

There are scary bits.
"Aargh!"

Lino suggests Harry goes
to sit in the Reading Room.

At last, Harry is so gripped by the story, he's too busy reading to make any noise. There is peace and quiet in Opposite Town.

Until...

"Good afternoon!" shouts Toto as he walks through the door.

"Quiet please," says Lino.

"Pardon? Can't hear you!" yells Toto.

Do you know why Toto can't hear?

"Shhhhhh!!!!"

No-one has ever heard Toto speak so loudly before.

"What's wrong?" asks Toto.

"You're too loud," laughs Harry, and takes the earmuffs off Toto's ears.

"Oh, that's better," says Toto.
"I'd forgotten about those."

But Harry isn't listening.
He's reading his book.

Quietly.

Harry and Toto are always finding opposites. If you enjoyed reading Quiet and Loud then look out for the other Opposite Stories.

Stop and **Go**
Created by Paul Shuttleworth

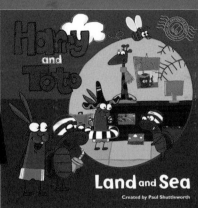

Land and **Sea**
Created by Paul Shuttleworth

Empty and **Full**
Created by Paul Shuttleworth

Available from all good bookshops and Gillie the Giraffe's online store
www.harryandtoto.com